BE
at
WAR

Battle for Love

RIKAH THOMAS

BE

at

WAR

Battle for Love

To:
Anfernee
Such a joy seeing
you and sharing smiles
& joy!
I hope you enjoy
the book
Blessings-
Rikah
Thomas
10/1/19

RIKAH THOMAS

BE at WAR: ***Battle for Love***

Published by Ink & Paint Publishing

ISBN: 9781693914379

 This is a work of fiction. Names, characters, businesses, places, events, locales, and incidents are either the products of the author's imagination or used in a fictitious manner. Any resemblance to actual persons, living or dead, or actual events is purely coincidental.

Scripture quotations are taken from BibleGateway.com and are under public domain in the United States.

Cover Design: Jessica R. Sanchez
Interior Images: Pixabay Free—released under the Creative Commons CC0.

OTHER BOOKS

BY

RIKAH THOMAS

Heavenly Ink

Follow Rikah Thomas at:

www.rikahthomas.com

www.instagram.com/rikahhope

www.facebook.rikahthomas

DEDICATION

Here's to all who have traveled life within the alliance of marriage. You know the sacrifice, love, and commitment it takes to become one flesh, while growing independently into the person you were each meant to be.

This book is written with all of the symbolism, heart, thought, emotion, and discovery of what marriage must often go through to fulfill its eternal purpose of revealing God's love here on earth.

Here's to loving our partner in life well, and together helping each other finish the race set before us.

"...Pursue righteousness, godliness, faith, love, endurance and gentleness. Fight the good fight of the faith. Take hold of the eternal life to which you were called when you made your good confession in the presence of many witnesses."

1 Timothy 6:11-12

(Oils on canvas)

Let our souls dance under the stars as we reach for the moon; and when we fall short, let Love light up the darkness—keeping us dancing under stars of Grace.

Rikah Thomas

BABY GIRL

A cold day in early December, Minnesota breezes are blowing with the assurance of snow. The promise of a white Christmas looming.

The labor pains start, and the womb that carried this little life these past months moans in discomfort. Clenching her teeth, face askew with the deep agony of a contraction, the young mother fights against her body. It wants desperately to force this little human out of the cocoon, forever exposing it to the elements of life—the good, bad, and in-betweens.

Push. Breathe. Groan. Push some more.

Effectively, the final strain sends the bundle of flesh through the canal and into the light.

Taking the first breath, her newborn lungs eject a curdling scream. Blood pulsates through the cord, clothing her lily-white flesh with bright red liquid. The twine of existence, so wonderfully knit together by a loving God, declares life wins this day.

The day of her birth. Divine. Appointed. Celebrated.

Emma is her name.

From the corner of the room, hidden behind the spiritual veil, evil makes a note to keep an eye on this small, unassuming, and unimportant infant.

BABY BOY

Another day in the Caribbean welcomes tropical rain, drenching the small island. It pours down on galvanized roofing, sounding like horses thundering down the road in the bright early morning. The birds cry out from within the coconut trees as the animals awaken to the screaming of his small newborn voice.

His chocolate brown skin flaunts a beautiful glow under the humid sunshine, radiantly sneaking through the flower curtains and slatted glass panels that create the window. He, too, is wonderfully knit together by a loving God, who declares this day that his life wins.

His mother frowns. Her concern consumes her, wondering whether he will be strong enough to make it through the day. The roosters and piglets bask in the joy of the fresh air, and her worry grows. She sends out his sibling to get the goat's milk she hopes will soothe his hunger. He cries for fullness and comfort.

The day of his birth. Divine. Appointed. Celebrated.

Jacob is his name.

From the corner of the humid and sunny room, hidden behind the spiritual veil, evil commands his watchmen to keep an eye on this small, struggling infant.

CHOSEN - EMMA

Years pass quickly.

At the local fair the little white, freckled-faced girl stands with a gentle soul and a tender heart. She waits patiently in line for her turn on the old-fashioned horse and carriage ride, wondering what excitement waits for her. She is glad that no one from home ever inquires about where she is going. The sign above the tent communicates words that make her heart joyful. *All are welcome, and something magical lies ahead.* She stands on tiptoes, her excitement on display for all to see, anticipating the unknown. *Something magical!*

Finally, the gravel crunches underneath the weight of wooden rims. The ride stops, and she jumps inside the four-wheel wooden carriage. It's covered with her favorite colors as if it was designed and painted just for her. Unbeknownst to her young mind, there is an inscription engraved into the teal and orange bench. It declares:

This one is Mine. She is special. I will favor her, and she will know My Spirit well. She will possess My heart of love for others.

The tan colored conductor (who takes the tickets and drives the ride) with thick, black, curly hair smiles and winks, and tells her to buckle up. With gentleness, he snaps the reins to get the white and chestnut horses moving. Expectation fills her. Somehow, she is aware that this moment will reveal an important nugget of knowledge for her future.

He prepares her for the journey, impressing upon her how essential it is for her to view this time of reflection through his eyes. He promises to be gentle, but warns her of the impending truth that this will hurt. A jolt of fear rises up, and her heart beats faster.

“Let go. Trust. Believe.” He breathes out the simple, yet seemingly impossible words.

As the clear blue sky begins to darken, clouds swirl in their grayness like an angry eel twisting and turning. The reels of an imaginary movie clip begin to roll against the backdrop of the moody stratosphere. The redheaded beauty is fascinated.

His ability to show the past, present, and future transcends her childish human perspective, but she hangs on anyway. Something compels her to keep watching as her fearful heart craves to see “more.”

As they embark on a supernatural journey, the magical horse drawn carriage takes Emma through many of her formative years, where promises prove false. Life hurts. Her past experiences trample on her dreams in the same way the horses trample the ground. The ride stops at very precise points on her life’s short timeline. There were many points when choices were made for her—ones that she didn’t always understand or want. Painful junctures when another piece of her peace was stolen without care or concern.

In and out of the chaotic jaunt between earth and heaven, the trip reminds her that life was harsh. There were no magical ponies to save the day back then, and certainly none now—not like these beauties pulling her along.

Disappointed at being reminded of the pain, she wonders how to stop this ride, which is turning out to be not so fun after all. Even if it eventually lands somewhere divine, or is "magical" as advertised, it's not what she expected. *I wanted a little excitement and joy*, she thinks, *not to remember the sadness always lingering beneath my happy face.*

As if he could read her mind, the driver overrides the current images. New visions encourage her. They display the same timelines, but the perspective is astoundingly different. She realizes that through the chaos, there was always a loving guide. That guide never left her side.

The Spirit of God, hovering over each moment, was always watching down from heaven as each life event came and went. *He was brokenhearted too.* He wept *with* her as her innocent heart shattered from the abuse, neglect, and refusal of others to love. The multiple divorces of her parents and step parents, and the continual abandonment she felt, afflicted his heart too. The arrow of loneliness deeply piercing their hearts as one.

The Spirit witnessed how others' selfish decisions crushed her. He loved her during her own foolish choices too, even as those choices cried out in obscurity and justifiably condemned her. Yet, his love changed everything, completely retelling the story of her failures.

Watching in the carriage's rearview mirror as they sail past the cloudy visions, the images say it all. They show her continuously falling short in relationships and personal goals. Her stunted identity feeds her delusions from the root of unworthiness running deep inside her soul. Emma weeps.

She can't bring herself to believe the Spirit's forgiving and merciful declaration of grace. She was hurt by others so deeply. She too is guilty of much harm, causing pain to others as well. Even the unthinkable; a life taken in the wake of fear, her turn to forsake the innocent. Now her memory calls out the name she took as her own. Murderer. Harlot. Not enough.

The enemy presents himself, familiar with her from years of surveillance. He tries to hijack the ride; hijack her mind. He assaults her peace with his weapon of shame, the dagger of accusations plunged into her fleshly conscience. Emma doesn't resist. She deserves to be hated. She half-way hates herself.

Salty water wells up in her hazel eyes. She withdraws to the corner of the wagon, tears streaming down. As the stern words within her mind rage upon her sensitive heart, the condemnation boils. Like bile rising in her throat, she feels self-loathing and contempt escalating. She hears the words, clear as trumpets in a church. *You will never be enough. You are a horrible human being.* The phrase echoes from her past as if the experiences were happening right now.

How great her collapse. A miscarried dream brought forth from a lie.

Sinner. Ugly. Hypocrite. Liar. Nothing.

She slides down further into the seat, feeling powerless in her whirlpool of disgrace. Who can save her from herself?

Who loves her enough to take the guilt, shame, and pain, and carry it for her?

Where is Emma's ally in this battle for her healing and peace?

The darkness envelops her, and the deep loneliness and isolation reminds her she must battle for her own wellbeing and sanity. No one cares about her or her scars.

Emma begins to drown under her sorrow.

In an instant, the conductor speaks and Emma remembers a moment from her youth; a word of promise spoken over her. *She was destined for more.* A whisper in the quiet of the night from a God she had only heard about.

In spite of the battlefield scenes, now plentiful with demons of regret and angels of hope, Emma dares to dream with optimism. As the foes take up arms, she determines to fight back and look beyond her past, believing her heart of love can free her. Her strategy—make the enemy believe that no matter what he throws at her, she is strong enough to overcome it.

As the last tear falls, the conductor commands peace to cover her soul. He places a shield of protection over her heart to shelter her from the pain of remembrance as he drops her back off at the gate. He winks and smiles one last time, filling her soul with a miraculous joy. It replaces the sting of the ride's remorse. Emma contemplates what just happened and wonders: *will I see him again?*

CHOSEN - JACOB

He rises early, his deep brown skin glowing under the bright sunshine as humid warmth already causes him to sweat. It is time to feed the animals and run his errands. Showering in the yard afterward, he takes his tan colored pants to dress for school, which he hopes he can attend this morning.

Incredibly bright minded and smart, he falls behind in his studies. His sadness goes deep, regretting that his young life must be consumed with grown-up cares. On the surface, his eyes shine bright to hide the truth—the pain deep within him. He gives *denial* permission to keep him safe from others as he hides his true self. His strategy—make the enemy believe he cannot be affected by his present circumstances.

Thinking about the day and his mother's usual absence, he questions what his future will hold. Thoughts interrupted, he comes back to reality knowing he must once again forfeit his opportunity of schooling for the sake of the family's livelihood. He must again tend to their garden, pulling the potential sales of fruits and vegetables from the lush ground. No learning today. "Earn his keep" he's told, while his child-must-be-an-adult heart grows heavy.

Half satisfied with the sweetened milk and piece of bread meant to sustain his small frame for the day, he heads out. With a quiet soul, he longs for something more that even he doesn't know.

As Jacob waits in line for the usual town bus, he notices a different one approaching. *That's interesting*.

Cautious and untrusting, he jumps on as the conductor (the person who collects the fees for the ride) throws open the side door. Before him, the bus sign supernaturally changes the destination on the front windshield.

"Buckle up, please. Your magical ride will commence—past, present, and future."

The conductor smiles and winks. His glowing tan face asks Jacob if he's ready to be stirred up, kindly directing him to take his seat. Thinking the back row is best for keeping an eye on everyone, Jacob heads to the rear and slides into the brown leather, double-wide seat. Defiantly, he mutters, "No, Mr. Conductor. I won't be stirred up."

Jacob notices the wordy inscription etched into the window. The proclamation reads:

This one is Mine. He is special. I will favor him, and he will know My Spirit well. He will possess My heart and passion. He will learn of Me, believe, and spread My truth to others.

Before he can oppose, the driver has put the bus into gear. Now it is flying high through the air. Gripping the sides of the seat to keep from smashing into the rear metal door, Jacob opens his eyes wide, unappreciative of his lack of control.

The images of his short life flash before him in gray swirls outside the window. He wonders if anyone else can see this picture from below. He hopes not; he doesn't want to be recognized. He detests any attention or others knowing his business.

Jacob sees his past young face endure the loneliness, frustrations, and people that make up his world. A rude comment here, neglect there, knowing that deep inside he must protect and care for himself. This boy, sweet as his chocolate color, hates the truth of being alone. Yet, he desires nothing else.

Living life in solitude, unavoidably amongst others, is a double-edged sword he must wield as he wages his personal war of self-protection, while advancing his goals. Jacob knows he can either resist his bend toward avoidance or succumb to the powerlessness of wanting to be near others. He is fully aware of his disdain for them because of their broken emotional baggage, so the conflicting tension between need and want continues to dump his sensitive battle-blood on the ground. He believes that people don't care. He, in fact, no longer cares.

The sky reveals the next scene, a hand flying back to meet him on the side of his face. *Whack!* Punishment for something said. *Shriek!* Yelled at for being a kid. His countenance doesn't change, but he pulls himself within, vowing no one will ever own him. No one will cause him pain. No one.

Little by little, his emotions entrenched within, become more calloused each day. He resists the tears, mastering them with his strong will. He promises himself that no one will see him cry, and he hides the anguish in his heart as the last tear rolls down.

The last one. Ever.

The Spirit takes him through the years, which were specifically orchestrated just for him. It stops at the places where choices are made for him, ones that he didn't always understand, nor want. In and out of island life, it appears that only rejection meets his needs and demands—to leave him alone. The mistakes of others and their egocentric, in-lieu-of-love offerings, given to anyone but him, remind him that he doesn't matter.

The enemy, who has been observing him since birth, shoots a mortar, hoping to blow up his confidence with a weapon of rejection. The accusations are thrust into his fleshly conscience, telling him that he will never be enough. The labels float through his mind. They remind him of his failures.

They call out his name: Uneducated. Poor. Thief. Not enough. Unworthy.

The conductor senses he must jump in and rescue him from spiraling into hostile territory, for Jacob's emotions are too fragile, unaware of their hidden strength. Waving his hand over him, he commands, "Peace!"

It is then that Jacob remembers a moment from his youth. A word of promise spoken over him that he was created for more. Coming to him as a whisper in the quiet of the night from a God he had only heard about.

Winning the mental scrimmage, he hopes for a better future. Strategically, he deliberates on how he can remain isolated, and yet still obtain what he needs to construct a different life. Always the achiever. The Lone Ranger.

This little boy dreams of more and believes his ability to make things happen can take him there. Only he can't bring himself to accept the love of God's Great Spirit. He cannot love himself. So who can save him?

Who loves him enough to take the guilt, shame, and pain, and carry it for him?

While Jacob hides behind a hardened look, the conductor drops him off. He winks and smiles one last time, miraculously filling the young man's heart with excitement, a feeling foreign and uncomfortable for him. All will be well tomorrow. Jacob ponders over what just happened. *What does all of this mean?*

PROPHESY

Out of eternity, God calls from His throne and states: *"In the near future, I will bind these two souls together. Beyond color, temperament, personality and culture. Beyond failure, weaknesses, and limitations.*

Before the appointed time, it will be necessary for them to know the agony of soul which comes from wrestling with faith, and asking the hard questions of life. It will lead them to Me. And in that hour, after the years of their preparation, this boy and this girl of destiny will meet. It is assured.

To My heavenly messengers, I say, 'Go, and with purpose, uproot Jacob and Emma's worlds. Let the earthquake of dysfunctional comfort shift their religious foundation to ensue spiritual movement. Leave them disillusioned and hurting. Allow their misplaced trust of the world to be questioned and let circumstances ignite a deep longing for Me, contradicting what others will pledge to rescue them in the wake of discontentment and turmoil. A false hope.'

It is important that the enemy take them for granted. He must be falsely confident of their defeat as he declares his ignorant war on them. The struggle that the rival fuels will deceive them, requiring all of deception's artillery, intentionally creating enmity between My chosen and the condemned.

For it is then that I will deliver Jacob and Emma. It will happen at the precise time. My angels will provide the truth and comfort they need to push onward, but only after they suffer the refining fire, fully ablaze to remove the impurity of compromise.

They will hear My voice and draw close to My presence. Faith will be born. Upon hearing the invitation to surrender their strong wills to My love, they will bend as unblemished gold in the goldsmith's hand. Pure gold within the flames, proving itself pure; authentic faith suffering, to prove itself true. Nothing will ever be the same; Jacob and Emma are forever Mine."

SAVED

In time, the young woman finds her way to God. He reaches out for her as she walks on the pier, and the overcast clouds reflect the darkness in her soul. Finally, at the end of herself and the years of compromise and chasing love and significance, Emma pours out her prayers to the God who captivates her heart.

She vows to follow Him. *"Loving God in heaven, the road has been long of false beliefs and lost perspective of myself, You, others, and where I belong. The unhealthy need for approval and endless searching for who I am is getting old. Exhausting. A dead end.*

Lord, the turmoil and strife are too heavy to carry alone. I've done all I can to make sense of the world and to save myself. To no avail. To still be lost. God, I surrender my heart and life to You. I commit to trusting You and believe that You are the way, the truth, and the life. I confess my sins of seeking love in the people and things of this world, as if that would redeem me from my pit. I repent of my ways. Lord Jesus, I am Yours."

In time, the young man finds his way to God as God reaches out for him. He saunters into the gathering where the Friday night movie is playing on the side of a building. The gangs on the film are at war, and their misplaced internal conflict is ready for combat. A man jumps in, unafraid, offering a message of hope. Extending to each member a way out of the fighting. Life over death.

Hearing the message of hope and possibilities for a greater future, Jacob knows he needs this same forgiveness. He needs a second chance. The weight of his lost identity and deeds crushes his conscience.

He vows in simplicity to follow Him. *"God, I don't know You, but I want to. I hear that You can save me from myself and give me a hope and a future. I have tried to live my life on my own terms, believing my ways are the best, and that I am enough. But I am wrong. I am unable to save myself. God, I believe You are true, and I am willing to follow You, to live my life in a way that pleases You. I give you control over my heart and life and ask that You save me."*

God's prophecy of yesterday commands truth to stand firm, agitating the great liar, and the enemy cringes at the destiny-shattering conquest in the heavens. Angelic hosts rejoice and shout their praise, while the adversary, in hate, vows to use everything in his arsenal for their eternal destruction.

The enemy spews forth in anger. *"Use all of the depraved spirits needed, or their own fleshly brokenness; whatever it takes!"*

He will hold nothing back—spiritual weapons of war, demons of iniquity, haters of all that is good—to destroy his rivals.

Evil's hate unravels, the thread of contention being sown into the battle of rage, while Emma and Jacob make their leap of faith from opposite ends of the world. Heaven rejoices over confessed salvation on earth and dances to the music of victory.

They are His.

TESTED

From heaven, the Lord gives His decree to the Host of Heaven's Armies:

"Now that they are Mine, give them room to learn of Me. Open wide the rivers of life and opportunities. For through every hardship and test permitted, they will hunger for the truth and grow spiritually stronger.

Do not interfere with My loving trials designed for them. They must stumble and fall, even fail, for I am sifting their character for a greater work. I am removing their fleshly selfishness, pride, and stubbornness of heart. If left untouched, these traits could hinder them later when the battle is at the height of its purpose.

Until I unite them, death to their false self-image will come through the necessary confusion of faith. But they will always have the opportunity to choose between Me and the world, and through the conflict of flesh and spirit, they will learn to distinguish the difference between unbelief and compromise versus faith and obedience. As they make their way through the enemy's traps, I will never leave them or forsake them.

As they experience suffering, My instructions will be a shining light in their darkness. The pathway will become clear in the valley of death, and My truth will be as sweet as honeycomb to their souls. When they seek Me with their whole heart, mind, soul, and strength, their true identity—the pure self, found only in Me—will be embraced, and unwavering trust will flourish mightily amid the battle.

I am walking close and holding them tightly under the shadow of My wing. I am their shelter, protecting them from the inevitable crossfires of sin.

Throughout their journey, there will be numerous fleshly and spiritual victories and failures. Their breakthroughs will lead them to a higher ground of faith, despite the downfalls that sin painfully invites. In the face of compromise, many souls will be eternally rescued because of their testimony, and their fight to live out My righteousness will break their hearts over their unintentional betrayal of Me and My ways by the choices they make.

Their devotion will hang in the balance as the adversary longs to take them out of the game. He will lie and attempt to deceive them of their deeper calling, which is when I will bring them together in holy union.

In that divine moment, I will bring Jacob and Emma together. A couple crafted by My hand, prepared for each other. An alliance of love and faith for laboring together in life and ministry, they will build their world in innocence and a family in naivety.

I will bestow on Jacob and Emma the sanctification of marriage. It is My gift—a sacred space to discover love and enjoy passion, being held close in safety and solidarity. It is where vulnerability, authenticity, and intimacy are honorable and satisfying. As spouses, friends, lovers, and companions, they will fight the good fight of love and marriage, for love is war.

And when the storms of life threaten to annihilate their world, they will exemplify My love, grace, and mercy when it is needed most. They will have the eye of their heart opened and grasp the true treasure of commitment and forgiveness.

It is then that Jacob and Emma will be unstoppable. Confidence and power from on high will open wide the floodgates of blessing and fortify the way.

My Word and My Spirit will hold them up when they feel overwhelmed and discouraged in the heat of the battle. And when the waters rage and threaten to drown them in hopelessness and despair, this noble couple will stand strong.

Though arrows of turmoil attempt to wreak emotional destruction, and they are bruised and battered by the demon grenades of doubt and hate, they will not be stopped. I will be the weapon of their warfare, allowing this anointed duo to heal from the assaults.

The beautiful death to their fleshly natures will bring life through their momentary afflictions. Resurrection power will rise in their relationship for they will be more than conquerors through Me, who gives them strength.

Defeating their sin and unrighteousness with the weapons of brokenness and repentance, they will lead others out of the darkness and into the glorious light. Redemption will be unleashed, and the thread of salvation secured.

Fighting side-by-side, Jacob and Emma will remain steadfast allies of the faith—a prevailing and invincible spiritual might against the prince of darkness.

Evil's demise...only a matter of time."

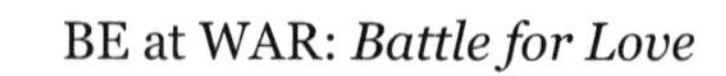

WILLING - EMMA

It's been years since Emma found her faith. Now, sitting in the classroom, she tries to think about the writing assignment in front of her. She has to share about this faith journey and what got her here. The past nine months in the training program have been the most life-changing experience she has known. And now, through the many diverse spiritual encounters she had in the desert and mountains, she is aware that the healing power of God is crushing old emotional obstacles in her soul. He is constantly revealing more of Himself and His will for her as she prays, seeks, and commits to new adventures.

There are a million tiny factors, so how is she going to share them in a few paragraphs? Even with a full book, how could she adequately describe the highs, lows, and intense struggles that led her to this moment? Yet, now is the time to take a giant leap of faith to fulfill her long-ago dream of leaving her mark on the world.

As Emma ponders, she's not sure how to write the story in a way that doesn't sound ridiculous. Feelings that God wants her to go to another country to live and help others is kind of confusing, even to her. Especially in light of the reality that she can't support herself, and she doesn't have a place to live or people she knows once she gets there. How can this be the invitation to *go*?

The only thing certain is she loves God and loves people. A big marshmallow heart on legs. She smiles.

How does she portray on a page every vital decision she made over the past year in hope and fear? To sum up this unexplainable adventure called faith? *Help me Lord.*

Head down, pen to paper, she starts to write her heart out.

Lord, when you brought that man to speak to the class last week, and he mentioned his ministry in the Caribbean, my heart burned within me. It's like I know You want me to go there!

After years of waiting on You and growing in my faith through each success and failure, I see a pathway in front of me. I am excited to keep in touch with him and his wife and learn more about the people there.

I am willing to go Lord. I am crying out, "Send me!" My compassion and care have grown over the years, leaving me yearning to make a difference and to love others well for You.

I sense You asking me to trust You in greater ways—for my provision, purpose, and future, the very things I already long to do. Lord, hear my soul cry in this poem as I write it to You. Please make Your way sure.

I AM A PUZZLE PIECE – By Emma

I am watching my life as a jigsaw puzzle, put together by the hand of my God.

I am unaware of the complete picture; yet, I see the beauty, reality, and purpose in His divine intervention as He places me where I belong.

Piece by piece, I am transformed.

My heart is still as I do not want to rush the final picture's reveal, or hasten its form in hopes of fulfilling my perceived destiny sooner.

I don't have to stress over the unknown.

I know it is not beneficial to manufacture in the flesh what the Spirit of God is creating, for I would rather wait to see the image in its beautiful entirety as God lays it all down, one piece at a time.

Only then is it perfection.

So, I leave the finished product to God alone.

In this moment, I see the fragments of preparation and call. Tomorrow, however, may be the time for me to go and begin the adventure. Make me ready, Lord. Send me.

Yes Lord, send me.

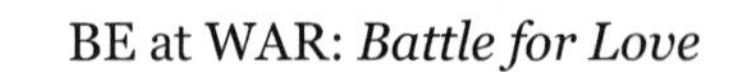

BLESSED

From His throne, the Lord gives His blessing over their lives:

"Young Jacob, a bright risk-taking-adventurer, will not hesitate to follow Me and obey Me fully. I will move faith mountains with him, this island boy I have called from birth. And after he has been sifted, he will return, stronger than he ever dreamt possible.

In humility, Jacob will impact eternity and many will come to know Me through his testimony of brokenness, redemption, and authentic transformation. His logic and hard work will reflect My courage and strength.

Emma's tender heart toward him of grace and patience will be like nothing he has ever known. Though he will fight against her love, he will come to know it as My heart for him.

She will shower him with My tangible love through her unconditional love and forgiveness. He will take her under his wing and desire to protect her from the world, reflecting My love for her.

Emma will be a woman who loves Me intensely and follows Me to the ends of the earth. Her eye will be quick to see what I see, and her ear swift to listen for My voice. Many will know My love because of her, and though that love demands of her selflessness and suffering, her joy will return to her in full. I will pour out My courage as a sword of strength to rescue, shelter, and restore her.

As the war rages on between heaven and earth, I will keep Jacob from collapsing under the stress of wandering in his personal desert, where soul thirst and hunger consume him. After he conquers the evil in pursuit, he will help her fight her battles by bringing My peace and truth to her wayward feelings.

Jacob and Emma will have everything they need to follow Me, love each other, and serve My Church. They will use their gifts—past, present, and future—for My glory. Nothing will stop them. Even the darkest nights of temptation and failure will ultimately bring life and resurrection for them and others.

I will use their inadequacies, mistakes, and grief for My good. Their lives will be broken bread and poured out wine. My glory and My favor will rest upon them until the day I summon them home into My loving arms. Nothing will be wasted. Nothing discarded.

My Word is as reliable as the sun rising in the East and setting in the West. As immovable as the ocean within a hurricane's wrathful pathway are My promises. I have spoken them, and they will be."

WILLING - JACOB

Another Sunday morning finds Jacob at the church building in his village. The roosters are crowing, and the people are starting to awaken.

He goes to his mind's tranquil place, while he sweeps the wooden floor of the small building. As the morning breeze comes through the screen-less windows, mosquitos start feasting on flesh. The sun is warm and comforting, shining through and inviting him to imagine a life far away from here.

Jacob wonders when the next group will be arriving from the States. His pastor invited him to be part of the ministry opportunities that are coming, getting Jacob excited for the work God is doing. He is also happy to hear that a woman the pastor met senses God wants her to visit the island and serve with them. It sounds like a promising trip, and encourages Jacob to keep dreaming about when he might be able to travel and experience his own spiritual adventure.

As he reflects on earlier years, Jacob is thankful that he has changed greatly over the years. It's been a long time since he saw the life-changing movie in the village. And now, God is stirring up his heart in anticipation of the future, as people and events fall into place on his behalf. The past is gone, and his longtime dreams of youth are getting closer to becoming a reality.

He wonders if the new group will bring their church some food items (like peanut butter, cookies, candy, and snacks) that they cannot buy on the island. It's always nice to receive donations and try new things.

He prays while he sweeps.

Lord, You have transformed so much of my heart and life. I know there is still more work to be done with my trust of others and letting people know me and help me, but I thank You for the opportunity to still be of service in this community.

You know I love You. You know I long for more in my life, more than what is available here. I get anxious, wondering what can be. But for today, I am thankful for the privilege to sweep Your church floor, and take care of the things that need attention.

Life has prepared me well, and You have used my childhood to teach me to work hard, to have a resilient attitude, and to keep my perspective in the challenges. I sincerely hope this isn't where it ends.

I am willing to go and serve wherever You take me, to make a greater impact on the world. Please utilize me in grander ways. Please don't let my life be meaningless.

Lord, use me.

FAITH

The Lord witnesses their movement as they fumble through the day-to-day, aware of the earthly choices they wrestle.

Alone in their search for tomorrow, Jacob and Emma wait for God to open a door. He hears their sincere prayers, even as they grow impatient. The temptation to doubt if God really said what they believe He did weighs heavy on their minds.

Sovereignly, God speaks of the future:

"Despite her past and the many sins she commits, Emma returns to Me. Believing that doing anything for love is worth the cost, she repents, and I hear her petition. With great love, I heal her heart with a gentle touch.

This will be the time of her resolve, and in the healing, she will learn to create works of inspiration on paper and canvas—sharing Me through the stories I give her and the pictures she paints. She will touch many lives with her acts of service, worship of Me, and loving well.

Jacob will start businesses and provide for My people through his talents, experiences, and abilities. This woman and man of faith will be equally gifted and equally matched for Kingdom purposes. Shining bright in a dark world that needs the hope and resurrection power of My Presence, their obedience will effect mountains of oppression. The void of emptiness that fills the hearts of men will be saturated with My living water, impacting eternity.

Leaving family and friends several journeys over, they will put their trust solely in Me. For a time, life will be good, and their faith will soar high as the fulfilment of a dream appears to manifest. Their flesh will be forgotten in the wake of spiritual victories—each church launched, each business begun, each ministry birthed—leaving their egos exposed and vulnerable. It is then that Satan will sift them recurrently—with no mercy—attempting to confine them as prisoners of war.

He will accuse and condemn, but I will be the One to question. He will unsettle them, but I alone will conduct their souls' interrogations. Despite his plans and maneuverings, I will renounce the enemy. Every time he stands, impudent, I will chastise and reveal the hidden motive of the heart to offer a divine rescue plan.

As the heavens watch, God puts forth the challenge for the angels listening:

"Will Jacob and Emma run away when things get hard? Will they deny Me?

Will this couple choose the wide road of the world and its ways or the narrow one that leads to life?

Will Jacob remain fervently steadfast on the path I have chosen for him, even when the enemy lies, and they believe the other is the enemy?

Will Emma trust Me in the process, no matter how painful or dark it is, believing victory's light is near?

Will they stubbornly deny their love and abandon their vows to Me and each other?

Will they still believe what I spoke so long ago concerning their relationship and the good it will bring to others? Will they hold that promise tight when their eyes are blind, and their ears are deaf?

Will they conquer their demons, sent specifically to plant seeds of discord and sow despair—offering them a counterfeit life of compromise?

Will they see the lies for what they are?

Will they run toward the truth?

This is the race. This is the pain.

Choices. Consequences.

Sowing. Reaping. Casualties. More emotional bloodshed.

Decisions to be made—choosing life or becoming lost forever in death.

At the height of the battle, will they hold My word close? Will they draw their swords and put their protective spiritual armor back on—the very ones they ditched by the side of the road to chase a deceptive truce with the camouflaged enemy?

Will they endure, resting in the abundant life I left for them to discover? A scavenger hunt of the heart—hidden in My word, to be discovered through My Spirit, and experienced through My presence?

Will they fight the good fight of faith?"

Heaven declares the battle cry, holding nothing back from Jacob and Emma's arsenal for triumph.

Angels of power and strength form ranks.

Let the angelic hosts wield their weapons against the enemies of humanity—the demons of evil. Heavenly firepower of glory will shoot shells of grace and forgiveness to protect them. And the helmet of salvation, the sword of the Spirit, and the belt of truth will slay the foe as prayer and praise complete the full armor of faith; disclosing to the demons their inevitable and ignorant end.

Show the terrors of darkness their frailty, and the chink in their malevolent armor because they believe that Emma and Jacob's flaws will cause them to fall to their spiritual deaths, never to breathe new life again.

And know this, there is power in the name of the Holy One of Israel, and the God of heaven and earth is ready to defend.

Prepare the trumpets.

Sound the battle cry.

Charge!

REFLECTIONS - EMMA

The sandy waves invite a somewhat older Emma to come play. She puts her toes in the warm water, feeling sand massage her toes with gentle grit. It's a beautiful day to take a break from the routine of work and studies to revisit the ambitions for her future. She is no stranger to seeking and dreaming.

What does she want? Where is she going? It's been nothing but uncertainty awaiting a clear direction to move in, after the training program.

The bright sun guarantees a sunburn on her freckled skin. If only she cared enough to cover up. However, there are more pressing things to consider as Emma walks the beach, her mind mesmerized by a melody of crashing waves.

An open spot on the beach, amidst the assumed stay-at-home moms and their little ones, invites her to stake her claim. This is her time to play the part of scribe and journal precious thoughts. Times like these are her favorites. Nothing compares to this sweet, intimate way for her to seek God's will through prayer and writing.

Setting down her shoes so she may spread the bright orange towel, she plops herself down. Emma wiggles her butt deeper into the sand to make a comfy seat. This may take a while, digging up the core desires from her heart of long ago.

Pen and paper ready, she begins to surrender to the emotion threatening to spill over. The deep contemplation she held back, for fear of a meltdown, has arrived like the tide.

Her eyes fix on a prancing seagull that hopes she has a morsel for him to consume. She almost laughs at his hope. Hope is growing to be a bitter, unrealistic word.

Emma refocuses herself. With an inhale, her pen finds its mark, and the ink flows.

Lord, how long must I wait until you bring me the one I yearn for? I am sad over the years of being alone and watching my friends get married and have families.

I am being faithful as I bide my time, going to church and taking classes to learn more about You. To be honest, it seems to be taking so long.

Where are the promises I believed? Is this all You have for me? Am I just an average girl longing for the out-of-the-box fantasy life? Have I missed Your promptings and signs all these years?

What about that mystical state fair trip I took when I was younger, and that conductor who showed me my life. That was so real! Except even that vision seems to be distant and cold. Perhaps it was only a mirage in my lifelong desert.

Maybe the challenge is to be content where I am.

Nevertheless, I have dreams, and they don't let me rest. I still imagine my life in another country, doing the impossible.

What will my future turn out to be? I'm still young, but feel like I'm falling behind the successes of those I know. What's my problem? What's the delay?

Is my life crashing to a dead end like the waves, or being muddied like the sand between my toes? Is it going to inevitably get trashed like this beach from uncaring and unconcerned visitors? Will I ever be blessed with a husband to love and have children with? Will our love be faithful and run deep as we build a life together? As we share about You, Your love, Your sacrifice, and Your truths of eternity, will those we love listen?

I know I must let go of the past first, and the parents who don't care—the family who isn't there. I long to rewrite my understanding of family and what it means to be loved. Even replace my scarred and broken beliefs with more realistic concepts of what family is, and can be through the filter of Your gracious and unconditional love.

Wow, it's tough being young and wanting it all. Yet, stopping would be like obstructing the waves and wind from their movement right now. Simply impossible.

Please let the meditation of my heart and my choices be ones that draw me closer to You. I don't want to fall away as I have done in the past.

Lord, with the sea and sky as my witness, I commit to living my life for You. While I wait, I look to You and believe what You spoke in the secret places, until the vision is complete. I know You are faithful.

I love you Lord.

Letting the sunset mimic her thoughts, Emma is satisfied with the words now resting on her sheets of paper. As the last bright rays slide behind the horizon for the night, she tucks her desires into her notebook and whispers a prayer over them.

REDEMPTION

Looking forward, the Lord knows He must unshackle Jacob and Emma's mindsets before they meet. He must expand their limited understanding of the world they live in, and the religion they profess, while they struggle to believe for their future. They must learn the truth before their bondage of tainted mentalities and spiritual ignorance collide, and deception leads the way. It can cause them to stray off the divine pathway for their lives.

With a heart of compassion and mercy, God speaks truth into their soon-to-be earthly union. The hosts of angels listen intently. He proclaims the enemy's defeat once and for all in these soon-to-be young lovers' lives.

"When love gets old, and they are familiar with each other, the fires of refining will escalate into an inferno of immense proportions. Flying close to the flames will scorch them, but they will not be consumed. Because I am with them, they will not be devoured by the passion of worldly temptation and decisive betrayal, even though for a moment it will knock them down and cultivate disbelief of My love for them and their love for each other.

These chosen ones will wrestle with truth and fight to stumble upon a secure foothold within a now cracked foundation. But compromise will not master them, and all that the adversary throws in their path will only strengthen their resolve to walk closer with Me. Triumphantly, Jacob and Emma, will rise from the dust and ashes to light and glory.

Satan's twisted fingerprints: deception, treachery, manipulation of the flesh, striving, pride, ego, and doubt of Jacob and Emma's faith and religious endeavors will leave their marks. The foe will leave nothing untouched. All that concerns them will blow up from his missiles of doom: dreams, health, goals, finances, family, and ministry.

They are not exempt; rather, this man of faith and this woman of love are chosen.

Nevertheless, through all the burdens and battles of life: being man, woman, mother, father, husband, wife, and minister, I am here, enabling them to carry their heavy crosses of spiritual growth and personal revelation in My Power.

I will pull them out of the inferno before they are consumed by the flames. When they turn, repent, and come to Me in unity, they will be a force to be reckoned with. As I proclaimed, the sins of their youth will not drag them under; instead, it will push them forward from glory to glory, strength to strength.

I am giving them a double blessing.

My Spirit pours over them.

This is the time of their anointing.

This is the moment of truth and the purpose for the other incomprehensible moments. A divine instant in destiny.

Their sins are forgiven. Doors open that no man can shut. Through their testimony, My faithfulness and grace is revealed—hopeful evidence to a broken world. Then and there, Satan will double his efforts to constrain My beloved son and ruin My precious daughter.

From this day forward, they stand united, their love and commitment an impenetrable shelter. Their faith stronger, they will serve Me before kings and princes.

No more shame.

No more guilt.

No more condemnation.

No more lies and delusions.

No more defeat.

Only truth with love.

Only victory to overcome.

Let it be done.

The journey of the redeemed must continue.

I, the Lord, have spoken."

CONTEMPLATION - JACOB

It's a beautiful night to fish, which is one of Jacob's favorite things to do. Alone. No interruptions. No one telling him what to do, how to be, what to think. It's also a chance for him to get away from the family and the demands being voiced—*who is going to cook, who will do the wash, and where are all the little ones?*

The bright moon overhead promises a successful catch this evening. Barefoot, he steps over the huge rocks to get to his favorite spot. Coconut trees overhead, he listens to the rustling of the branches as small critters scale the limbs. *Maybe it's an iguana trying to nest for the night?*

Taking his fresh mini mackerel from earlier that day out of the bag, he attaches the bait to the hook. Tonight, he hopes for a snapper. His mouth waters as he imagines it fried and swimming in butter. He already knows how good it will taste.

Throwing back his arm and then flinging it forward, he releases the line. It sails freely through the air to the location he eyeballed from the road. It's known for being a profitable spot, and he wants all the scaly sea creatures he can get.

Jacob is thankful he's okay by himself and enjoys the solitude. It is one of the few opportunities to be left alone with his prayers and thoughts. It's in this moment his dreams can run wild without logic trying to reign them in, or his current reality squashing the what-could-be possibilities.

He is already overwhelmed at how long it seems to be taking for things to happen. His mind wanders and his eyes stare off into the distance, not really paying attention to whether his line is catching anything. His thoughts replay past conversations he's had with God.

Lord God, what do You have for me on this island? It's all I know Lord, but it's not all I want. I am enjoying my job, and I'm thankful for the ability to work and get my own place soon. But what more is there for me?

God, you know the constant attacks and strife living in this place. It's so difficult to rise above the mindset and culture that doesn't believe I can become more than I am. Thankfully, I'm not afraid to engage in combat and fight with the truth, but sometimes, I forget what the truth is.

It seems so far away. My mind and my choices are the battlefield during this season of my life. One foot in the church, one in the world.

The wind blows as his line tugs a little, implying there may be a fish on the line struggling for its freedom.

I wonder if I will ever marry. Have a family? Will my dreams to own my own business and earn enough for my own place ever happen? Is it even possible for someone like me? Am I too dark, classified by stereotypes and judgements? Am I too uneducated by the world's standard?

At least I am thankful to work in Your small church, God. I am happy to clean and prepare for Sunday's gathering. But is that my only purpose?

What do You say?

Jacob hears the gentle, whispering winds, "Wait."

Wait? For what? He muses.

Wait.

For who?

He thinks of the team coming from the States in a few weeks and the preparations that the pastor and church are organizing in anticipation. The missionary couple is excited. Together, they look forward to meeting the new group.

What will they do this time? Paint houses or put in water pipes? Perhaps go around the island for a tour? Or will they experience the usual visit to the waterfalls so they can say they jumped off a cliff? Or hold the brown and gold boas that wrap themselves around the trees, near the water?

Whatever it is, he's thankful to be a part of it.

Wait and see.

CONNECTION

It's been a long time since Jacob and Emma felt God speaking to them from their separate corners of the world—calling them to a greater purpose. But God proved true and every man proved a liar as they moved toward God, and always unknowingly, towards each other.

Some bet against the dreams and visions they shared. Who did they think they were, believing for more with their meager beginnings and current insignificant realities? But they did not give up any ground. Excited about imminent opportunities, the two faith walkers fought for themselves. Against the hostilities of the world. Against all odds.

Time does what it does, tick-tock, onward. The prophetic word, indeed sent from heaven, blooms right before them by the hand of God. Their destiny reaches for them, pulling them into their future.

The future is here.

Emma steps off the plane, conquering her battles of doubt, financial struggles, and conflicting cares just to arrive. She recalls the fight of faith and obedience it took to continually show up to the meetings for this long awaited adventure—to trust God for the money, to leave her job, and to believe He had more for her in this place of the unknown.

All of it comes to fruition as she steps out of her comfort zone and exits the plane, believing God for this exact promise. Exhausted from the long trip and prior months of preparation, she longs for relief and her body aches for a bed to fall asleep in.

On the terminal ramp, Jacob sees her coming out of the plane door, attempting to hold her black rectangular gym bag. It looks heavy, so she drags and kicks it in front of her. He smiles, watching her determination to conquer it; she is a woman of strength. The promises of God come back to him, reminding him of his prayer the past few months—seeking God, desiring what awaits him in the future.

Wait and see My son. Wait and see.

Her ankle length peach dress and red curly thick hair, loose and flowing, make his heart skip a beat. Jacob smiles with the quiet confidence that she is his promise. She is meeting him here. The *yes* resounds in his spirit, soul, and body. It is undeniable—she is to be his wife one day soon.

Emma doesn't know it then, but he is her promise too, sent by God to greet her and be the man to carry her life as he carries the heavy gym bag.

As Emma walks down the steps onto the ramp, she lifts her head and looks into his dark brown eyes. They twinkle with a smile as their gazes connect. Eternity sighs with satisfaction, knowing this long-awaited moment is complete.

Her eyes light up and spark as his smile broadens to say hello. For a split-second, time waits for their spirits to impress upon each other—this is something big.

He offers his assistance. She accepts.

The beginning of a lifelong story pens its first word as the beginning of a union made in heaven lands safely on earth.

God wins.

ONENESS

And so Jacob and Emma's journey goes. Courting. Sharing. Talking. Unveiled hearts exposing their contents.

Lives meeting in the middle of diverse cultures and experiences—they engage, letting God do His perfect work. They are excited to step out in young faith; their love for God the phenomenon they share. The joy of mutual revelation of faith and their life stories possesses them. With one spirit and one heart, they declare to the other, "I see you. I want to know you. I believe we are meant for more, together."

The ongoing heart-to-heart talks create a connection, and the desire to know each other establishes the familiarity they yearn for. Conversations, laughter, prayers, and intimacy, leads to asking more meaningful questions.

Who were you?

Who are you?

Who will you be?

I want to know it all.

Newness gives way to familiar, which only begs for a deeper level of commitment. Over the weeks, Emma must risk exposing her past broken emotions, understanding that to be fully loved is to be transparently known. But her sins, deep with crimson blood, reveal a heart afraid to be real. What if he can't accept her failure and is not able to love her now?

The devil sends a missile of recollection. From the past scenes of her life, comes a reminder of her weakness and folly—a slaying in a moment of deception and fear. A sin so dark she has spent years hiding its existence. How to share now, with this man she wants to trust and love. With this man God has so clearly said would be hers to create a life with and serve Him as one.

The enemy of her soul, the hater of God, reminds her of her shame. He taunts her. "You do not deserve love. You are worthless."

Fear and anxiety try to rear their ugly heads.

But grace wins out, and Jacob takes Emma's heart tenderly into his hands, vowing to love her. He commits to being the vessel of God's love, truth, grace, and forgiveness toward her. He pledges to forsake all others and keep her safe, believing she is made for more. Holding her close, he boldly states his love can be her confidence and strength.

His words offer her unconditional acceptance. *"He loves you. I love you. He forgives you. I forgive you."*

It's Jacob's turn. His secrets torment him, and he is unsure of how to reveal himself to her without fear of rejection. His insecurity from childhood experiences and labels from a culture that defines value by shades of color haunts him. What if she sees his faults and weaknesses of character? Will she love him? Will she accept him?

The rival of Jacob's soul, the hater of God, reminds him of his inadequacies. He mocks him. "You are not enough. You don't have what it takes to succeed. No one will take you seriously."

But grace wins out, and Emma takes Jacob's heart tenderly into her hands, vowing to love him. She commits to being the vessel of God's love, truth, grace, and forgiveness toward him. She vows to forsake all others and to always believe in who he is and who he can become, committed to standing by his side and cheering him on.

Her words offer him unconditional acceptance. *"He loves you. I love you. He forgives you. I forgive you."*

The foe falls from a forceful wound. The weapon of forgiveness hitting its mark as innocent love says, "*I do.*" The swordplay is over, and they trust God just enough to step out and conceive a life together.

"I will be your wife."

"I will be your husband."

With a look of love and hope that the future will fulfill their hunger for what they lacked in youth, Emma and Jacob commit their devotion. Happiness has a moment to dance with them. Looking deeply into his eyes, hands grasping his fingertips, Emma's words flow.

"Jacob, I vow to God to be all I can be for you, here on earth as it is in heaven. I am committed to loving God and you with all my heart, mind, and soul. I promise to be faithful, loyal, and loving. Always renouncing others to be present with you. I promise to accept you in all the stages and seasons of your life and to believe the best about you.

Where I am weak or need to change, I promise to be open, to learn, grow, and be my best self for you. I am devoted to you and whatever life brings, always walking with you in it. Poor or Rich. Sick or well. Good or bad times. I am here to be your friend, lover, helper, encourager, partner, and companion for life.

I will fight for you, and with you, through all our battles as your confidant and ally. A defender and a guard. I am yours. I pledge you my love, care, support, and loyalty from this day forward. I love you Jacob. I will always love you."

Tears in his eyes, Jacob replies from the depth of his heart.

"Emma, I vow to God to be all I can be for you, here on earth as it is in heaven. I am committed to loving God and you with all my heart, mind, and soul. I promise to be faithful, loyal, and loving. Always forsaking others to be present with you.

Where I am weak or need to change, I promise to always be willing to learn and grow to be the best me I can be for you. I promise to accept you in all the stages and seasons of your life and to believe the best about you.

I am devoted to you, and whatever life brings I will walk with you in it. Poor or Rich. Sick or well. Good or bad times, I am here. I will be your friend, lover, protector, provider, partner, and companion for life. I will fight for you, and with you, through all future battles as your confidant and ally. I am yours. I pledge you my love, care, support, and loyalty from this day forward. I love you Emma. I will always love you."

Honest.

Loyal.

Supportive.

Dedicated.

United.

Married.

FUSION

United, Jacob and Emma lift their imaginative custom-made crosses to build their lives on, and follow their God. They do their best with the roles they devise. This is new to them. Having someone to share life with, to dream with, and to enjoy as their own treasure is the mountaintop experience they imagined possible long ago.

With devotion they take up each other's armor and place it on the one their heart loves. It is a painstaking process. Piece by piece, they intentionally cover each other's vulnerable and broken gaps of the soul. By faith, they prepare for the war they signed up to wage and win.

The war of love.

The war of marriage.

They waste no time fashioning their life. And doing whatever is necessary to meet their need of feeling like they are helping God, and making a difference in others. They live out their destiny, slowly achieving what they questioned was even possible for them to accomplish. Such a defective people with little in their wheelhouse of experience for such divine undertakings, and yet favor rests upon them. Their efforts produce success and bring glory to God.

Be a husband. Be a wife. Be a father. Be a mother. Say *I love you* and teach their family about God and life. These are the weapons of their warfare, and they do great damage to the enemy and his workers of iniquity simply by living out their faith with righteousness and integrity in the day-to-day demands.

They gladly forget their meager beginnings as they proceed on their journey. They no longer need to mention the loneliness of the past.

They vow to know better and to do better.

They forget what they didn't get to do or have because of fragmented pasts. Both are smart, bright, and witty. Sensitive and caring too, despite the world stomping on those tender places of their hearts. Now that they are together, the battlefield becomes easier to identify and conquer in spite of its multiple dimensions.

Where one is blind, the other has the ability to see behind the veil, revealing the dangerous blind-spot of the other. But it is a process to learn. They struggle to overcome the damage. The enemy tries to weaken their willing determination to grow and change. He reminds them of their warped patterns of brokenness, tossing random ugliness onto their path. If left unattended, the enemy grenades could rob the two lovers of all they build, beyond what they can imagine. Casualties and loss greater than anything the past could threaten to steal. The stakes are so much higher.

Jacob and Emma intentionally bury their wreckage—choosing to forget and move forward. They numb out the pain and disappointments to make new oaths, creating the code they now live by. Still, old habits from old hurts can cause new wounds.

Emma ponders old truths, her life motto: *I will do anything for love.*

Contemptuous, Jacob still believes: *I will not let anyone in, especially for love. No one will get close enough to hurt me.*

A fissure in the armor. A habit of bad perspective. They are both in danger.

The enemy hears and begins to applaud. He thinks he has gained back some ground, snatching the prophetic word away from them. He sends out his workers of iniquity, commanding them to watch for the hole in their emotional walls, where the demons can fire an assault on them and their family, a war started from before time.

His command is simple. Shoot to kill. Make them bleed. There are no rules when it comes to annihilation.

Oblivious, this couple smiles and laughs, expressing joy over being together. Onward, they fight the fight of youth and innocent love. Determined to press in and let go of what hinders them, they keep their eyes fixed on their General and obey the directives He gives through His written Word and His Spirit. They embrace their new life.

It is good.

Evil shakes its head at their ignorance. Have they learned nothing over the years? It knows the victory is too brief to be sweet.

Jacob and Emma must learn not to let their guard down, not even for a moment. They must engage in the spiritual and earthly fight steadfastly, for the true battleground is opening up before them. Blinded, they are oblivious that their sins, too numerous to count, desire to be resurrected from the tomb of forgiveness by the prowling devil.

He vows to consume them in the near future with acidic memories, wanting them to hide within their humanity as desperate fugitives and ineffective prisoners of war.

Then he has a chance to win.

Their battle has just begun...

Identity.

Sin.

Faith.

Fear.

Love.

Hate.

Marriage.

Division.

Truth.

Combatting the invisible enemy of their soul.

And he is ruthless.

While they are blind.

FAMILY

Life seems good to Jacob and Emma as it keeps moving forward, and their family grows. Emma realizes her now big belly is ready to give up the twins fighting for space in her womb. Opening the window in her kitchen to let the morning breeze in, she prays for strength to get through the pregnancy.

Jacob's words come back to her from their time snuggling on the couch last night. He is concerned about becoming a father and carrying the responsibility of his growing family. It keeps him up at night.

Prayer has become second nature for Emma as she whispers, *"Lord, thank you for blessing me with a man who thinks of his family and takes his role in our lives seriously. He is a good man. And I know, with Your help, he is more than able to love and care for us all. Bless his mind and heart with peace."*

As their terrier puppy crosses the tile floor, Emma bends over in pain, just as the water drips down her leg.

"Oh, ouch!" she gasps. She waddles over to her purse to get her cell phone and calls Jacob. The time has come to meet their babies. As rehearsed in the birthing classes, Emma fills up the birthing pool and prays for the contractions as pain picks up its pace.

"Ohhhh, breathe Emma. Breeeaatttheeee." She coaches herself through, keeping track of how far apart the death grips squeezing her womb are.

Many minutes later, the front door slams, rattling windows, and Jacob rushes into the kitchen with purpose.

"How are you feeling? Are you okay? Did you call the midwife?" His questions fall on preoccupied ears.

Helping Emma undress and ease into the warm water, he massages her shoulders and whispers a prayer for peace and a smooth birth into her ear.

She relaxes. Until the next contraction doubles her over, and she feels the need to push down. Looking at the clock, Emma is impressed that things are moving quickly. For their first baby, it is moving toward the six-hour mark of being in labor—*not bad*.

The midwife lets herself in and immediately gets to work. She is on a mission and needs very few instructions. They've all practiced this in the past several weeks, and now it's game day!

Emma begins to bear down, losing awareness of Jacob and the midwife. All she can think of is getting these long awaited prayed-for babies out; relieving the pressure and pain.

"Ahhhhhhhhhh!" Breathe. Pant. Release. Push.

Time feels deceiving. Appears to be moments, but one hour lapses into another.

"Urrrggggggggg! Oh God, please get these miracle babies *out*!"

One big push and Luke's black hair crowns. With a *schloop*, he falls into Jacob's hands, the water rinsing him off as Jacob lifts his chubby son to the surface. The midwife is quick to suction out his nose and mouth and ties his life cord so Jacob can cut it.

Wrapping his cream colored body in the mint green blanket, the midwife puts him into Emma's arms to hold while they wait for baby number two to make her appearance. Emma shifts her weight, cuddling her son close to her. Tears, so many tears of gratitude and love flow down her cheeks as she holds God's tangible grace to her body. Emotions stir up within Jacob, and he thanks God for this moment to behold his son who looks very much like himself.

The new mama pants through her mental prayer. *Oh, Sovereign Lord, I do not deserve this gift. I am so unworthy. And so thankful. Eternally and deeply grateful. The Lord bless you, Luke, my precious one.*

The contractions pick up speed, and Emma once again feels the urge to push life out into the world. Tired. Exhausted. She hands Luke to Jacob to hold. Desiring this moment to be over, she begins to rally and force herself to work with the pain, using it to bring their baby girl into their family.

"Arrrrgggggghhhhhhhhhhhhh" She sings the same tune she's been singing the past many hours, hoping for this one to pop out much quicker. Soon, her final push answers her prayers. Lilly slides out, a couple of ounces lighter than her twin brother.

Jacob lifts his baby girl out of the water, overwhelmed at the sight of his two beautiful children. Lilly begins to scream, letting them know she needs attention. Cord cut and peach colored blanket wrapped around her, the midwife helps Emma put Luke and Lilly at her breasts where they can nurse and rest.

Jacob and Emma look at each other at the same time, eyes locked. Smiles reach out for the hug they feel, but cannot give, and a lifetime seems to fly by as they both remember that gleaming look at the airport, when their eyes met and God's will became real.

As the twins nurse contentedly, another promise from heaven is fulfilled, and the angels sing.

BATTLE

Over more time, the life they dreamt about and the one that showed up reveals the void between hope and reality. They work hard to provide for their family.

They dream again of the future and what they don't have. They tend to forget from where they have come. Now, owning a business is hard work and doesn't always bring in what they need to meet their financial obligations. The relational and financial pressures squeeze what little bit of faith remains. Yet, they continue to help those who God brings their way, always trying to do and give more as the burdens grow.

Together, they work harder, always willing to sacrifice their needs and wants so God's message of love and grace can go out and offer hope. The boulders of responsibility for family, ministry, and careers bog Jacob and Emma down as they keep the plates spinning in the name of God and faith. God and faith, two ideals that are slowly getting lost in what seems real now, which are the past due notices plaguing their mailbox and the threat of foreclosure on the home they possess. They take on more, do more, become more, and believe their efforts can save what is theirs. All in the name of faith.

Soon, they are no different than those who labor long and hard for what seems urgent, losing sight of the important. Jacob and Emma assume they are okay and that their needs don't exist. Meanwhile, the internal needs of their souls beg for attention, missing each other. Missing God.

Years pass quickly—a blink of an eye.

This man and woman of faith watch their children grow up and become more distant as they pursue their independence and identities. Those who were born after the twins catch up with their siblings and crave the freedom to live their own lives.

Now a family with unique hurts and expectations, Satan knows exactly how to attack each individual member. The enemy inflicts maximum damage to one, so that one affects the group. The past and present neglected emotional and spiritual needs loom. Painful lessons knock on the door of their lives with annoying accuracy. The adversary never loses sight of his goal to seek, kill, and destroy these chosen ones of God. His targets are in sight, and his patience is paying off.

Reputations. Character defects. Issues of the heart. All is fair in war. Their unprotected and unaware minds are open for hunting season. The demons draw close for the final blow to their souls and destiny.

Division. Conflict. Offense. Unforgiveness. Don't care. Don't remember. Forget who you are. Forget God. Life is too hard. Believe the doubt.

The strong man, Jacob, turns to work night and day, numbing his needs. Or worse, declaring he has no needs. Emma begins to fear she is losing her love and longs for identity and purpose. Her joy of being a mom and raising her family because of her heart to obey and please God is gone. As the last one leaves home, the nest is now empty of the purpose and security she found and enjoyed.

The middle-aged woman from Minnesota and the middle-aged man from the Caribbean are both still drawn to "more." Not the "more" that thrilled them when they were young—that promised adventure and purpose as they trusted and followed God, but the "more" of independence and discontentment. Dysfunctional "more" that won't let the other in now for fear of loss and hurt. The "more" of the flesh and its selfish desires. The "more" that entices them to shut down and blame the unmet expectations and disappointments of love, family, church, and life for their issues.

Trying to avoid loss and hurt, they create more loss and hurt.

Justified.

Warped perceptions trickle down the hierarchy.

Their sons, so full of potential, don't know who they are and the enemy is close by to whisper the invitation into the world's distractions. The lies feed their need to belong. To dispute what color they are. To confuse their understanding of where they fit in. Despite their parent's affirmations and encouragement, they believe they are inadequate and defective. Have nothing to offer.

Diversity is now used as a weapon against them—part of their story, but not part of their true self. It rages on in their young souls, presenting as contempt. As another arrow flies through the air, the enemy's aim remains perfect. Be angry. Don't trust. Rebel.

Their daughters hide behind internally self-inflicted silence. Demons battle their confused minds, making them believe they are not enough. Terrors whisper, *"Compare yourself to the world. You fall short. Not skinny enough. Not pretty enough. Not perfect enough."*

For one beautiful daughter, the cuts on her skin are cuts to her soul. She bleeds for love, acceptance, and answers to her private hell. The others search for the love they think will make them whole, digging around the dumpsters of unnamed sinister places to beg for it from nameless immoral people.

The attention they crave, though priceless, is sold cheaply to them by scumbags who don't care.

Sibling rivalry wars against them. Their differences wound like bullets shot at them from the elated devil. They judge each other with their actions and haughty looks, screaming out, *"You're not worthy enough for you are not me. Ugly. Stupid. Unlovable."*

The enemy thinks he's won. A house divided. A marriage in trouble. A man lost. A woman tormented. And children wandering away from the light into the night shadows of the soul.

Evil waits for their world to fall, so proud of himself.

Liar.

Thief.

Murderer.

Accuser.

Deceiver.

Cheater.

CHAOS

Emma storms out of the kitchen, temper rising like one of her menopausal hot flashes. All she can think about is how unempathetic he can be toward her feelings and needs.

He is so stubborn and selfish!

Reminded of their first years of marriage, her heart sinks. She feels so insignificant—even now, after all these years together.

What happened to God, me, and then everyone else?

Emma's annoyance ruminates on memories of their life after the kids moved out. A life of disconnection and aloneness. Her heart's desire was to simply reconnect with Jacob in the hopes they could once again rekindle their romance and love as a couple. So she asked for more time together and to do things where they could experience some fun. She even pleaded for a "we" thing, which they could explore and have in common.

It didn't go over well. She lost that battle, like many others before. His stubbornness resisting her because of his perception of being demanded of, when he didn't want to meet that demand. He didn't see things the same way and thought the way they lived life was just fine.

He enjoyed his work.

He enjoyed the tasks.

This was who he was, and he liked that.

But, this wasn't the way she thought marriage should be. Or the way she envisioned they would be. Admittedly, one of her goals was to stay connected so they wouldn't become a statistic during the empty nester season, the way so many articles said. The opportunity for disconnection, and even divorce, occurred at higher odds if they weren't careful.

She loved him too much. She had to be careful.

The thought of losing him was too painful.

He was her first love.

The spirit of fear latched on to that thought and got excited over the fruit of insecurity, doubt, and striving for control.

Emma's rants don't stop. *"How in the hell does he not get that our time together is important?!"* She declares in a huff, pacing in her bedroom.

"He knows that I need connection with him and don't enjoy being by myself every waking moment! He knows how I have pleaded for his attention and time for so many years."

She was so proud of herself too, reading articles and books to help her appeal to his love language and needs, imagining her efforts would attract him and make him feel her love. That somehow she would be noticed, appreciated, and the love reciprocal.

But it was not.

Demons all around sense they are at odds, celebrating their anger and frustration. Jacob and Emma are right where they want them to be.

Believe each other is the enemy.

Believe the other is hostile and unreasonable.

Jacob paces in the back yard, completely baffled at what just took place. He debates with himself, the lawyer in him arguing both sides of the situation.

"Doesn't she see all that I have on my plate?! The long hours and working so hard to meet the needs of the church and our family. Doesn't she know how exhausted I am? Can't she see that I have nothing left to give?"

Nothing. To anyone.

His court-room voice gains momentum. *"Why does she ALWAYS make everything such a big deal?*

Why can't she appreciate the time we do get? Why does she have to ask me for more when I am already doing all I can? She doesn't really care about me. It's always about her or the kids.

She gets the real me. She knows I love her deeply. Why isn't that enough? I came home wanting to see her and hear how her day went, but here we go again. What I didn't do. What I didn't say. She knows I need time to myself, what is so difficult to understand about giving me a little space?

This isn't the way I pictured marriage. It's not what I thought I was signing up for. It's too hard."

Jacob's heart beats with anxiety and irritation at believing he is misunderstood and judged wrongly. Again. He just wanted to come home, see his wife, and relax. So he convinces himself, for the truth could hurt, that he actually longs to be alone. He would be just fine.

It would not be today, though.

He thinks back to long ago. *When did things get so complicated and 'not okay.'*

Wickedness smiles, thrilled at their passionate discontentment and individual deliberation that they may not work as a couple anymore. Their love may not be the beautiful love story they always believed it to be. Maybe God didn't orchestrate their meeting and bring them together for a divine purpose. Maybe they have never been the perfect puzzle pieces joined together by a divine plan.

Emma and Jacob are right where chaos wants them to be.

Disbelieve love.

Doubt hope.

Distrust faith.

Evil whispers. "Run!"

Emma grabs her car keys and heads for the door. Jacob walks out of the side gate in the yard and turns down the street.

Evil celebrates its own victory with a corrupt smile.

DELIVERANCE

Taking their hands in His, God pulls Emma and Jacob out of the mire and the muck of life's war zone.

"ENOUGH!" He shouts.

The one true God, merciful and full of love commands, "*Enough. No more.*"

A gentle wind swirls about as He imparts His power into their weary and discouraged bodies. He wants to create in them new life, hitting the reset button of hope and restoration as only He is able. He longs to affirm them of what is true.

Jacob and Emma feel like they are in a daydream. A mighty supernatural force from heaven fills them. They rise to their feet. The vision encompasses them. This anointed and called couple begin to see how they lost their way. God woos them back to the gentleness of living out His rhythms of grace.

As they stand before Him on earth, surrounded by a vision in a field of sunflowers, God plays the movie of their life together. He wants them to see, so they can regroup, get perspective, and strategize for the final battle of their souls.

God reveals Himself to them and shares His heart. As His glory fills the skies, His warmth seems to comfort and clothe them.

"You have fought diligently and now is the day of reckoning. I will reward your faithfulness and restore your perspective. The veil is now removed from your eyes.

Where you were once blind, now you see clearly. I am opening the eye of your heart. Embrace my wisdom and eternal truth.

You must remember the path you started long ago. You must believe the journey of faith that is continuing. Nothing has changed. I have not changed. My purpose for you is not new. Watch and see."

Jacob and Emma focus on the images flashing before them in the blue sunrise sky. They are mesmerized.

Not willing to give up so easily, an arrow of the enemy flies to disrupt, distract, and destroy. It breaks in midair, falling to the ground. Frantic, Satan fires more angry darts in rapid succession towards them. They cannot be allowed to advance, for he knows the eternal impact they will bring. The great deceiver is losing his footing.

Malevolence screams. *"Leave nothing untouched! Challenge Jacob's pride and the image he so desperately tries to keep in check by his own double standard. Cause his integrity and reputation of good to be questioned. Let there be no doubt in his mind that he is unworthy, undeserving, and falling short."*

It almost works, and the little-boy-now-man feels his resolve melting under the condemnation. Then the Spirit of God intervenes in prayer, and the faith-filled man gains strength as God breathes more life into his bones with redemption's peace. Jacob will never be the same. This devoted servant, now a product of repentance, redemption, and grace is rising to his rightful place.

Leader.

Servant of God most high.

King.

Angry, Satan shifts his aim. The great opponent calls in his legions of demons, commanding them to attack Emma without mercy.

"Afflict her heart and mind! Leave nothing untouched! Inflict wounds so deep, nothing can soothe the pain. Where she once trusted and believed love, let nothing but doubt and despair cause her to question her identity and the worth of her soul. Tempt her to forsake love. Let there be only certainty that as she compares herself, she believes she is unlovable, unwanted, and abandoned with no one to care for her."

Jesus prays for them, speaking life through His intercession. As in days of old, the resilient woman of faith rebukes the attack, regaining strength as God breathes life into her bones of repentance, redemption, and grace.

Emma will never be the same.

Woman of grace.

Servant of God.

Queen.

Jacob and Emma embrace the revelation, resolving their minds and hearts to accept truth. They cannot explain the intense peace, and as they sigh deeply in surrender, their eyes land on the tan smiling conductor standing off to the side.

He winks at them, nods, and grins.

They smile as they grasp each other's hand in mutual understanding of what is to come and what must be done.

REFLECTIONS

Still holding hands, Jacob and Emma watch the moments frozen in time as the pictures reveal the past they ignored. From scene to scene the images change focus as God displays what He desires to show them. He wants them to watch, learn, and be humbled by the truth they lost sight of in their earthly concerns and fleshly cares.

First, Jacob watches. He is taken to a very painful and critical moment in their lives. The space in time where his heart hardened, and his mistrust wanted to protect itself. He was unwilling to love her well and meet the needs she desperately spoke of. He believed she asked for too much.

He sees the instrument of Satan's trickery coming for his wife. His beloved. The one his heart loves. The great liar approaches Emma with his charm and delusional words, flattering her with his snaked tongue.

She is mine, Jacob's heart screams.

He cries out for her deliverance, for mercy to intervene and stop her pain and the path of death she is on.

"Abba Father, help her! As she walks near the tumultuous shoreline of temptation. She is blind and willingly dipping her toes into the muck of sin, soon to drown. She has lost her way and doesn't know it.

Send the light to shine in the darkness of her soul. She has forgotten You, God. She has forgotten her face in the mirror. She has forgotten mine. She has dishonored her vow.

Send down the rain to remind her that You catch her tears and mingle them with Your grace. Open her eyes!"

His heart breaking, head cast down, he sobs. He hates remembering. Torn between the pain of betrayal and the hope of love, Jacob surrenders to the power of hope.

The film shifts to Emma. She is drawn to the frame where her beloved's face is. The sadness in his eyes reveals his own temptation and questioning of faith. What is real? Has any of this been real? Love. Care. Family. Hope. Purpose. Vision. Unity. Was it ever possible? No longer a young naive boy, the man wrestles with his identity and who he is. Midlife. Lostness. More doubt.

He is going under. Jacob, who believed he was made for "more" and that he was born for "more" is under attack. The visionary who hardened his heart early on, so no one could hurt him, is losing battleground.

She pleads for her beloved. *"God, save him!"*

Her heart is for him. It was always for him, even when he didn't trust or believe. She feels the burden he carries. So much pain. So many years of him pushing against the door of his heart to keep it closed and locked.

"Oh, God, give him grace."

How she longs to hold him and assure him of victory.

Her heart breaks for Jacob as she prays for his rescue.

She understands his struggles all too well, for her own soul reveals she too is melting under their mutual rival's attacks. The years of compromise encompass the hurt.

She too hates remembering the battles they've waged and the wars they seemed to have lost.

Eyes opened, hearts exposed, they get a glimpse of the struggle and love of the other.

Jacob sees the tender heart of his true love as it echoes forgiveness on the walls of air and clouds, desperately pleading for him.

Emma sees him driving in the rain, crying out through tears of love and faithfulness. He is desperate for her. He misses her and entreats God on her behalf.

God hears the plea and releases an angel from heaven. The doors they pushed closed, locked, and sealed all these years, are blown open so the Spirit of Truth can enter in.

She remembers her own longing, desiring his attention. Begging to be noticed. Missing him, she aches for connection and the opportunity to lavish him with love. A love without suspicion and doubt. Without him pushing her away.

He realizes how she holds his heart in her hands with such tenderness and protection, just like when they first met, and weeps at the lessons he had to learn the hard way. Sad over his own lies and betrayal, he looks away in shame and guilt.

Then, it is his own broken body bowing before the Father, asking God to take this cup of suffering from him.

"O God, please protect the heart of the one I love. Don't let her hurt. Don't let my choices break her heart. God forgive me and please protect her."

Emma's reflections of her sin and brokenness beg God to take this cup of affliction away.

"O God, please protect the one I love. Don't let him hurt. Don't let what I have done break his heart. God forgive me and please protect him."

The movie is paused.

The enemy shrinks back, unsure, as he alone watches the ending unfold.

The warriors of faith begin to understand the weapons of their warfare and the urgency of the future battles. They recommit to the war they began so long ago, and with new awareness vow to shake off all that hinders their race of faith, or threatens to disqualify them from the eternal prize they were destined to attain. From this day forward they will live a life of faithfulness to the One who saved them, and to each other. They will battle with eyes wide open, and endeavor to live in the world, blameless.

Onward.

Live.

Thrive.

Believe.

Never Settle.

Remember.

Fight.

RELENTLESS

As they press on, they continue the battle for their lives. And now one flesh, they are overcomers throughout careers, ministries, businesses, children, grandchildren, and marriage's healing grace.

One love.

One purpose.

One spirit.

Jacob and Emma advance in years, and as warriors of the faith, observe their wrinkled faces and the glimmer of wisdom and strength that sparkles in their aging eyes. They are grateful for the constant love, acceptance, hope, forgiveness, grace, and mercy that permeates their existence.

Not a perfect love, but a love that doesn't quit.

A love that stays true no matter the cost and the lessons to be learned.

A love that covers a multitude of sin.

A love willing to bear the pain of forgiveness.

A love that believes the best of each other.

A love that wants what God wants for themselves and for each other.

A love willing to sacrifice.

A love honored to lay down their life for the other.

God's eyes lovingly fall on Emma. His compassion for her reveals how He carried her in the darkest times, when she was torn apart by the loves of her life—her husband and her children. As a loving Father, He understands her inner turmoil and the conflict over how to love and accept them, while enduring the pain inflicted from their choices and perceived rejection.

Storms brew in a new attack, enticing Jacob and Emma to look further into the past. A plague of memory—the darkest of clouds—swirl around her soul. She recalls feeling alone. Abandoned. Rejected. Only longing to gather her family together under the shadow of God's loving wings. Her mother-heart breaks. Her lover's-heart is crushed. Why must she always feel like the one to choose? Would they choose her?

Her heart belongs to each of them, caring about them and wanting to protect and hold them close while they fight to be set free.

Their free will; her living hell.

Her only solace in the pain is that they don't give up. Not as a couple. Not as a family. They remain cemented in their devotion and commitment to God and each other. Once again, God sends his armies to their rescue through her prayers. Together, they stomp on the enemy's evil plans to destroy their good name.

They continue watching the battle scenes flash through the clouds. Bullets fly through the air and cut deep into their flesh. They fight on. The bombs put off black smoke. The enemy calls out his demon's names to remind Jacob and Emma of past failures and hidden shame, in hopes they will despair of life and choose to quit the intense battle of love.

Still determined, the two pick up their weapons and wage new warfare against the enemy. The Lord covers them with His gracious right hand as they push through the storms of emotional hail and spiritual winds blowing harshly. This is life. This is the great high calling—joining together in marriage. *Til death do us part.* Choose love. Choose devotion. Choose commitment. Choose faithfulness. Choose to honor the vow of long ago.

Cut and bruised, they grasp each other's hands with strength and fortitude. Shrinking back is not an option. Hand to the plow, they push onward. Always onward. And the heavens shout out their praise to the God who keeps them from falling.

Each scene shows their broken souls and crushed spirits when the enemy tries to sabotage their faith and wreck their family. He tries too many times to count throughout the years.

Arrows flying, demons yelling, Satan's workers race over to assist in the destruction of Jacob and Emma's bond. Their home. Their life. Those hellions try all they can to dig their talons into human flesh with their jagged teeth, desiring to snuff out their love, faith, commitment, and trust. But every time, God surrounds Emma and Jacob with His shield and protection, even when they thought they were failing and stumbling from faithless and disloyal choices.

Jacob and Emma begin to remember the conflicts as they watch intently. They see the angel of God never leaves them. His mighty sword is forever drawn, while the hosts of heaven's angels wield their weapons to fight for Jacob and Emma's victory. With divine intervention, they fight hard, defiantly persistent in always moving forward.

Captivated, they continue watching.

"Forward!" she cries. *"Through the building of our family and the birth of our children. Forward through the difficulties of planting churches and serving diverse cultures, and continuing to sacrifice for the opportunity to extend the spiritual invitations through earthly needs being met.*

Forward through the temptations of being human and of wanting ego and pride to get what it wants. Attention. Deception. Wealth. Prosperity. Lust of the flesh. And the pride of life. Our humanity trying to hide behind religion and the power of the law, killing the grace we do not fully understand.

The battle rages on. We see, though our flesh bleeds and our bones break; we don't let go of each other. We don't stop carrying our crosses either.

The cross of our conviction that God remains true when we are all liars. The cross of love and forgiveness that is unmovable. And even if sin justifies the bitterness that haunts the heart, the cross that shed the blood of redemption desperately holds on to the creed of faith. So, we carry the cross of commitment and dedication, even if others fail and people judge wrongly to vindicate their abandonment. We continue to carry the cross of truth that God is enough, whether we have little or much.

We never abandon the One our heart loves. We don't give up on each other, even when we fall down from sin's direct hit and are blinded by deception. Seemingly broken beyond repair from life's great disappointments, we fight on.

We do not cease battling for each other: Interceding, speaking truth, declaring our love, and dragging each other to safety when that is all it seems we can do. Our love of God and each other is the shelter from mass destruction.

We are also blessed to witness that after each battle, we bandage the wounds in prayer and clothe our bodies and minds with His healing Words of life. Holding each other close, we whisper promises that we won't quit the race of faith. We won't quit on our love. For we are no longer ignorant, nor innocent.

Love covering a multitude of sin.

Forgiveness always the weapon most effective to take out the enemy, despite his hope to kill off our fragile beliefs by the lure of false love. It is agonizing to watch.

The love of the world.

The love of the flesh.

The love of spiritual death.

A cancerous counterfeit—evil always tries to make deceptive promises seem real, as if they are what God created and wants us to follow.

Adultery.

Greed.

Dishonest gain.

Lies.

Games.

Ditch the ministry.

Chase the world.

We didn't concede, though we did at times fail.

Devastated, we remember that the righteous fall down seven times and get back up.

Glory to God. We always got back up."

FORGIVENESS

Glimpsing into the former years, they continue to pray, repent, and beg for mercy for themselves and their beloved.

Emma's supplication is multifaceted. Regret and loss rising to the surface.

"Oh God, heal this man I love of the harm that I have caused him. That was not my heart starting out on this journey of love, marriage, and serving You. I never meant to fail either of you or cause damage through my brokenness. I have learned so much about myself and what it means to follow You with my whole heart. What it means to truly love others with Your selfless love.

I now am aware of my selfish ways and the unrealistic burdens I placed on others. I needed to grow in unconditional acceptance and faithfulness over the years. I am grateful You loved me enough to crush me, and not leave me in the darkness of false love and expectations based on my pride and sense of justice. Lord, I repent and receive Your perfect love and forgiveness for me."

Jacob's words wash over her as she listens.

"Oh God, heal this woman I love of the harm that I have caused her. That was not my heart starting on this journey of love, marriage, and serving You. I never meant to fall short and break down the life we desired to build by my brokenness.

I have learned so much about myself and what it means to follow You with my whole heart. I see the pride and arrogance I have carried around, like a vagrant with his trash bag filled with trinkets. There was always a better way, the abundant life way, and I missed it for so many years because of my unwillingness to change.

I am grateful You loved me enough to crush me and not leave me in the darkness of pride. I confess my wayward heart to You, Lord, and I receive Your unconditional and constant love and forgiveness for me."

In the stillness where hearts are humbled, God speaks: "*Though your sins are as scarlet, they are as white as snow. I have separated you from all your sins against Me and against each other. They are as far as the East is from the West. Can you receive and embrace the freedom I am offering?*

I forgive.

You forgive.

Grant mercy.

Time to let go.

Time to allow forgiveness to finish its perfect work.

Time to relinquish yesterday.

Time to welcome healing's gift.

Time to lay down your grief.

Time to embrace renewed joy and peace.

Time for new beginnings.

Time for freedom.

Grace wins."

ONWARD

It has been years since God interrupted Jacob and Emma's life with a heavenly viewing of their faith film. Now, their eternal destination bids them to come. Death to the flesh. Life in the Spirit.

Glorious.

Worth the warring.

It is time to go home and leave behind their earthly purpose, work, and the loves of their life—their beloved children.

They have endured.

Now, they must press on toward the throne of God. As they walk to the open gate, they hear angels singing in the distance.

Jacob and Emma's desire for eternity intensifies. So many conflicting thoughts.

We feel unworthy, the earth-bound battles still fresh, a year like a moment in heaven. We aren't sure we deserve to be here, and yet, we remember the cross of Christ and that it is His righteousness the Father sees in us. We need a little more faith to finish the journey.

"98 years," Emma ponders in her plea. We made it 98 years—wars, battles, victories, and losses. The world and the enemy were unable to keep us down and defeat our love for God and each other.

She remembers the difficult path.

It was such a long time to be locked within this fleshly skin of humanity, warring against its urges and wants. Controlled at times by sin's pull, hurting those we love, hurting ourselves the most.

Grace beckoned us to shake off the shame and guilt as we staggered through the often meaningless and mundane days.

We were so often desperate and emotionally naked, believing that our sins had found us out. Exposed, we defended ourselves by hiding deeper into ourselves. Hiding in the world. Hiding in the church. We hid from those we loved. We hid, or the pain would have been too much to bear, tempting us to quit. Praise God for His unending strength and power to sustain us!

With each step forward, Jacob and Emma feel their superficial covering peel off. It is the stripping away of false selves and the emerging of their true selves. They are becoming more glorified than a thousand languages worth of words can explain. The dredge of sin's nature, now in fragments, flows away into the grace giving River of Life. The righteousness in Christ that tried to rise in the power of the Spirit so many times before is fiercer. Determined. Constant. Through surrender, they fight to finish the race like never before.

They lost some battles, it's true, but they also won a few with holy vigor and resolve. They look at each other with genuine acceptance and victory, knowing their destiny on earth as man and wife is almost over. Time to transcend to the greater passion of eternity.

As they walk, limping with old bones and aging flesh, they recognize each other in the twinkle of their mature eyes. It is a special look they are very familiar with. One that reveals; *I see you. I know you. And every hurdle we conquered; every opportunity we took to forgive and accept each other, all became God's tangible love and mercy.*

This was always the plan. Oh how fickle and foolish youth can be. She smiles at the simplicity of the truth. It is bittersweet, the joy of living life together and now being required to let go to take hold of their future glory.

There is no choice.

His glory.

Our glory.

Pure.

Whole.

Fully knowing and fully known.

Perfected children of Christ.

So close.

His light shines over them.

Jacob looks at Emma and speaks his truth with his eloquent words.

"I have always loved you, Emma. Even when I didn't know how. When I didn't trust. When I couldn't let go. Even when I failed, and my humanity won for the moment, my affections and mind were yours. You had my heart even when I wasn't yet made whole from the loss and brokenness of my own life.

I know you took a chance to love me. Often it was not easy. Nevertheless, I want you to know that I felt loved by you. A love I longed for from my youth, and in you that love became real. I have loved no one the way I have loved you. You were my first experience of grace. You gave me a deeper kind of acceptance and kindness, especially in the moments I believed I didn't deserve it. I am forever thankful for you and the life we shared. I was always your love. You were always my deepest love."

Her expression echoes his.

"I have always loved you, Jacob. Even when I didn't know how. When I didn't trust, when I couldn't let go. Even when I failed you, I was always yours. You had my heart when I wasn't yet made whole from the loss and brokenness of my life.

Thank you for choosing me to spend your life with. For opening your heart to me, trusting me, and being willing to know me. I have loved no other the way I have loved you. You were the first time I experienced God's grace. You helped me experience a deeper kind of acceptance and love, especially in the moments when I believed I didn't deserve it. I am forever thankful for you and the life we shared. My love belonged to you, and you were always my deepest love."

On the sidelines, angels and demons alike wait for the final word from above. Who will get the next command to intercede? Will it be trial or victory ushering in the completion of this final battle?

Angels start to sing. Evil turns to flee.

CROSSES

They move toward the light, hands still fastened together and dragging the crosses that seem extremely heavy now. Wasn't it only a moment ago they were at the airport, meeting for the first time? The warmth of Emma's touch comforts like so many times in the past. The familiar feel of her fingers against his, the way his hand fits perfectly into hers.

Years of practice with romance and selfless love are now a natural response to the nearness of their bodies. It is passion beyond simple consummation.

It is a divine connection, glorious and full of holy fire.

She reflects on the moments they shared such love—a soul connection.

Cherishing the way her legs would wrap around him, feeling desired by him. His tender kisses touch her face as he enfolds her in his arms. She gently tickles his back, very familiar with the softness of his skin. A look into her caring eyes invites the delicate kiss to her forehead, cheeks, and lips. His love is intense in its gentleness.

They know each other well. Affectionate. Attached. Loving. Needing. Wanting. Choosing. Absolute.

God permits them to listen in on their past heart-to-heart conversations as legs cross over each other and hands join together. They talk of life and love, their future together, and the fun and difficult times now gone.

Their conversations reveal the joy and laughter of simply being together. Even the struggles didn't hinder them from enjoying the quietness in each other's comfortable and safe company. Listening now, they appreciate the deep and thoughtful exchanges aroused within the lover's haven, and how they pondered the mysteries of their world with one mind and one heart.

Even with the tension of love and personality differences evident, they pressed into God and each other, praying for their communication, intimacy, friendship, and personal transformation.

There was so much good.

So many blessings.

So often hope.

Misty-eyed, they sigh.

Grateful.

Connected.

Intertwined.

Committed.

Satiated with love.

Devoted.

What a beautiful finality.

GLORY

The finish line is visible in the distance, and a heavenly glory lights up the sky. The earth is fading below, and only the promise of the Divine for finishing the race is in sight. Emma's heart overflows with joy as she is thankful for their journey.

We are in good company, that of Abraham and Moses, of Jacob and Isaac. From Adam and Eve to Jonah. The past 98 years now behind us are but a memory. It was real. It is a holy memory.

The *Jacob and Emma* movie comes to its close as they near the top of the mountain of God.

It is over.

The good. The bad. The love. The anger. The peace. The chaos. The laughter. The tears. The victories. The momentary defeats.

They did it. They ran their race. Individually. Together. They did not lose heart. When doubt filled them, they didn't turn back.

They did it—waging a lifelong war against the enemy of the world and their souls to stay close to Jesus. To believe His Word. To live it out. To shine on the earth. To proclaim the good news.

Whether in success or failure, they did it—remaining strong in their love for each other and persistent in their commitment to the truth of that love. They completed the work given to them.

Whether in ignorance or knowledge, Jacob and Emma ran the good race of faith. And now it is over. No longer pilgrims passing through, but children of God ready for rest. No longer man and wife, but the beloved of the Lord prepared for eternity.

They reach the top together; their past lifetime behind them for the generations after to tell. It will be a gift to learn from and be encouraged by. The message will be clear—it was NOT in vain. It all mattered. Earthly battles and victories for eternal rewards and spiritual impact.

One day, eternity will tell of the good things God did through it all.

As the heavens open wide, brilliant golds and yellows warm them with their presence. The desire to leave earth and enter into heaven is stronger than any sin or earthly pleasure could ever imagine.

They are given a moment to say goodbye.

Facing each other, a smile of familiarity, compassion, respect, and love flash like lightning through their gazes—electrifying mind, soul, strength, and heart.

They choose their final words with great reverence.

Emma's eyes cannot stop staring at Jacob. She echoes her past sentiment, knowing that this will be her last opportunity to share in their earthly bodies.

"I have loved no other the way I have loved you. Thank you for the kind of love that never gave up, always believed, and always protected."

Looking into her eyes, Jacob's words pour over her soul.

"I have loved no one the way I have loved you. Thank you for the kind of love that never lost hope, always believed, and always kept rising to overcome the darkness with the light."

He cups his hands around her face, pulling her close to him, gently putting his lips on hers. Years of kisses float around them like stars in the galaxy.

They linger, all the pain gone now.

Only grace, forgiveness, and mercy surround.

They share a unified, loving thought of their children and the legacy they leave. They trust God to bring them home safely, when it is time. They trust faith to remain immovable, knowing He will continue the work He has begun in their lives.

She pauses. *They don't want to let go of this moment. Not yet. It will never be the same. This time they have shared will be over, forever.*

She weeps.

He weeps.

"I love you, Jacob. You are my greatest love and my greatest sorrow. And I wouldn't change a thing."

"I love you, Emma. You are my greatest love and my greatest sorrow. And I wouldn't change a thing."

BEHOLD

Standing in the presence of LOVE, the Lord invites Emma forward. She stands, honored to present Jacob before Him.

"Lord, I present to You my beloved. He has loved You, God, with all of his heart and carried his banner high. Willing to sacrifice and follow You, no matter the cost. A man after Your heart, who never quit. Always fighting the battles to never forsake You throughout his lifetime. A man of integrity with a hunger for truth.

Thank You for allowing me the gift of sharing the path of redemption with him. I am eternally grateful and humbled over the moments we were together. I love him Lord, and he is Yours."

Jacob presents Emma, the one his soul loves, to the Father.

"Lord, I present to You my beloved. She has loved You, God, with all her heart and has carried her cross through the good and the dark times. A woman of grace and beauty she has loved well and has been a light for You. A woman who found favor with You and longed to please.

Thank You for allowing me to experience the path of redemption with her. I am eternally grateful and humbled over the moments we shared together. I love her God, and she is Yours."

As the radiant sun glows, the gates are opened wide and Jacob and Emma are held in the arms of LOVE. At last.

No more sorrow.

No more pain.

No more tears.

True abundant life.

Rest.

Love.

Peace.

Joy.

Wholeness.

Home.

Eternity.

The End

"We have fought the good fight. We have finished the race.
We have kept the faith."
2 Timothy 4:7

Love and marriage are not for the faint of heart. It takes a courage, bravery, and selflessness that few things in life may ever demand. And because we bring our innocence into this sacred relationship, we must be alert and learn that love has to often war against the flesh and misguided wills (a very real enemy of our souls) to triumph. Our ignorance of the battles of love can often inflict pain, and invite compromise from our blinded, unrealistic expectations.

Without a strong spiritual and healthy earthly perspective, we may spend precious time fighting for the wrong things—forcing a struggle for perceived individual freedom that separates our love and unity, rather than celebrating the joy and fulfillment it was designed to bring. Instead of becoming life-giving, satisfying, and rewarding, love and marriage can feel like a slow death of our individuality, dreams, and desires.

If not for the grace of God!

Love and marriage are worth fighting for, and the battlefield is this world we live in and the challenges we face as we learn life lessons, make mistakes, and conquer our false beliefs while attempting to build a life together.

This story is a fictional piece that opened my eyes to the beauty and possibilities of God's eternal vision of an earthly union. As my husband and I approached our 30th wedding anniversary, I was invited to reflect on our journey and celebrate the growth that often came through pain. At times, as I wrote this story, it was hard to look back because many times the suffering was in the dying to self, or the lack of it. It has not always been an easy road for both of us, but the rewards we are now enjoying have been worth the fight.

We celebrate that our eyes are opened (in greater capacity) to the deeper treasure that marriage can become, once we are willing to cooperate with His process of love, mercy, and grace. Through the example of God's unconditional love, we have grown to deeply appreciate each other and cherish what He implanted within us through the battles and victories of our marriage. Now, we are growing in our life together in a much deeper, richer, and beautifully connected way—authentically and whole heartedly—as we continue loving God and loving each other.

My prayer is that we are able to heed the invitation to fight for each other and our lives. Not shrinking back from the difficult battles of marriage or remain unwilling to learn the lifestyle of grace and forgiveness as we understand what is eternal and important. There is no greater victory or defeat in this world for us, our families, and the generations after us.

Marriage: A mystery to unravel and enjoy.

A joining of two souls on a journey toward God, themselves, and eternity.

An eternal gift of transformation.

An opportunity for God's love to be experienced by our spouse, through us, in tangible reality.

For it is only through Him that we are able to give and embrace this love the way He does: freely, humbly, unconditionally, generously, graciously, faithfully, passionately, unfailingly, and authentically.

It will always be:

Profound.

Confusing.

Rewarding.

Complex.

Worth it all.

Here's to love and marriage, and all that it is (with our eyes wide open), and all the beautiful possibilities it was perhaps meant to be this side of heaven.

Embrace and enjoy the adventure!

I would love to hear from you!

If you would like to share your story, you can email me at rikahthomas@cox.net.

Blessings & Peace

ACKNOWLEDGEMENTS

God: I love You with all of my heart, mind, soul, and strength. Your faithfulness, grace, and constant unfailing love are my source of joy and have healed my heart of much. You continue to lead me on a journey of wholeness and adventure, and I am excited about the future and what lies ahead. Thank You for trusting me with such a precious story regarding the union of marriage. It's a mystery I am still navigating, and yet I am forever grateful for the privilege of loving, being loved, and being called to deeper levels of Your love through forgiveness and grace.

Peter: It has taken me thirty years to truly grasp the depth of our love, commitment, and devotion to God and each other. We have built a very real, adventuresome, and solid life together through all the good and difficult moments, because we pressed into God individually and together, and remained devoted and committed to Him and our love.

I am so grateful for our many moments of laughter, fun, family, adventures, and the daily sharing of our hearts and thoughts. And I am thankful that we are able to eat the sweet fruit of our labor in these latter years. You are my lover, partner, friend, companion, and co-laborer for the Kingdom of God, and I am blessed then and now to enjoy a life with you and our children as we run our races. I am honored to be your wife and honored that you are my husband. I love you, and I am looking forward to the next thirty years with you and all that God has for us!

Tiffany V.: Thank you for diving into this project with me and helping make it better. I appreciate your commitment to excellence and the ability you have in speaking truth and cheering me on at the same time. It has been a joy working with you!

April and Tiffany H.: Another year passes and we are still going strong. Thank you for your friendship, for being my writing partners, and for helping make this writing journey a fun one even when it is often difficult. The hours spent sharing hearts, writing, critiquing, and inspiring each other to keep writing has been a precious gift in my life. Thank you!

Peter, Kamiah, Julie, Mark, and Dennis: Thank you for taking the time to proofread ***BE at WAR: Battle for Love*** and give me your input. I appreciated every thought, edit, and correction you gave so that this story can inspire and encourage those who read it. Thank you! I appreciate you!

Kenan and Kamiah: Thank you for being you. You get to be in here simply because you are my amazing children and I love you with all of my heart. Always.

Always Remember...

You are loved.

You are treasured.

You are valuable.

You are wanted.

You are unique.

You are meant to be different.

You are strong.

You matter.

You are enough.

You are meant to shine in this world!

Joyful sunflowers; they are happy to be themselves—dancing in the wind. (Oils on canvas)

PROMISES

The angels are now given the names of their next assignments. The Lord tells them to be kind to His precious ones and bring them safely through the fires and the storms of life.

He blesses and anoints His next chosen for the pathway of faith. He speaks the names of Jacob and Emma's children and grandchildren, declaring upon them redemption's way.

Radically and eternally saved.

BE
at
WAR
Battle for Love